KATIE'S WORLD

KATIE'S SWISS ADVENTURE

Karen Mezek

HARVEST HOUSE PUBLISHERS
Eugene, Oregon 97402

MRS. JULIA THOMPSEN

MR. JOHN McABE THOMPSEN

KATIE THOMPSEN

BETH McKINNEY

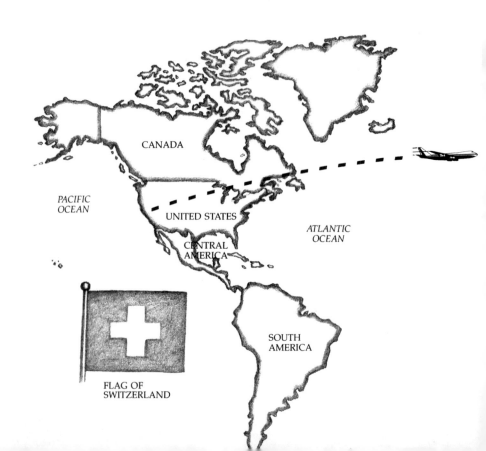

CANADA

PACIFIC
OCEAN

UNITED STATES

ATLANTIC
OCEAN

CENTRAL
AMERICA

SOUTH
AMERICA

FLAG OF
SWITZERLAND

PETER THOMPSEN

MRS. ALENKA HANOVER

DR. ANDREI KOPOLOV

KATIE'S SWISS ADVENTURE

Copyright © 1990 by Harvest House Publishers
Eugene, Oregon 97402

Library of Congress Cataloging-in-Publication Data

Mezek, Karen, 1956-
   Katie's Swiss adventure / Karen Mezek.
   Summary: During a visit to Geneva, Katie and her friend Beth spot a peculiar woman following
a noted Russian scientist and try to find out who she is and what she is doing.
  ISBN 0-89081-815-0
   [1. Geneva (Switzerland)—Fiction.   2. Mystery and detective stories.]   I. Title.
PZ7.M5748Kav   1990
[Fic]—dc20   90-33472
                                              CIP
                                              AC

Printed in the United States of America.

Chapter 1

Take Off!

"Oh, no!" cried Katie, rummaging through her bottom dresser drawer. "I can't find it anywhere!"

A huge suitcase appeared in the doorway. Behind it was her younger brother Peter. "You'll never find anything in that mess," he huffed. "Who cares about your dumb old diary anyway?"

Katie ignored him and continued her search, realizing she didn't have much time.

"Katie!" called her father. "What's keeping you? It's time to go."

"Please, *do* come," said her mother anxiously, making one last check to be sure all the lights were switched off and the shades pulled. "For once in our lives, we *must* leave on time!"

"Ahha!" Katie cried with relief, snatching the precious diary from beneath a pile of old school papers and letters. She stuffed it into her shoulder bag and raced down the stairs.

Excitement bubbled over as Katie jumped into the back seat of the family van beside her brother. Switzerland! They were going to Switzerland! Katie's father, John McAbe Thompsen, was a foreign correspondent and he was being sent on a special assignment to the United Nations. Katie wasn't exactly sure what the United Nations was, but she knew she would enjoy finding out.

"Pul—eeze let us come," Katie had begged when she found out about her father's trip. "We'll *never* complain. Or be late. Or be picky about food. Or be pests. Will we, Pete?" she added for emphasis.

"Very well," their father had agreed at last. "It will be an educational experience for you."

"And a test of endurance for us," added their mother, laughing as they both were smothered with hugs and kisses.

Now the day Katie and Peter had awaited so long had finally arrived and they were on their way. But they had one stop to make before

reaching the airport. The car turned onto a shady street, just two blocks from where the Thompsens lived, and pulled up in front of a cheery yellow house.

Before Mr. Thompsen had a chance to honk the horn, the front door flew open and out popped Katie's best friend, Beth McKinney, who was to accompany them on their trip.

"I'm coming, I'm coming!" squealed Beth excitedly. "I'm not late, am I? Will we miss the plane? Oooh!—I can't believe this is actually happening to me!"

Beth's mother and father followed her to the car. "Now take care, dear," said her mother, looking a trifle worried.

"Be good—and take lots of pictures!" her father called as the car pulled away.

Beth leaned out the window, waving frantically. "I will, I promise! Good-bye, good-bye!"

3

At the airport, Katie's father checked in their bags and showed the airline attendant their tickets and passports. Katie, Beth and Peter were all very proud of their passports. Katie only wished her picture had turned out better. The day they had been photographed she had dressed carefully and fixed her long dark hair in a ponytail. Then a terrible thing had happened. Katie had nice, twinkling green eyes, but the flash had made her blink. So glued forever inside her first passport, for all the world to see, was a picture of her with half-closed eyes and a half-opened mouth.

"You look sick," Peter had said when he saw it. "Weird and sick."

Beth's picture had turned out much better. Her brown eyes were wide open and both dimples showed. Besides, her brown curly hair looked wild and full, as if she had never, ever, in all her life, combed it.

At last, the moment came for them to board the plane. Mr. and Mrs. Thompsen and Peter sat together, with Peter by the window. Katie and Beth sat behind them, agreeing that Beth could sit by the window for the first half of the flight and Katie for the second half. As the plane lifted off the ground they felt their stomachs tingle and their ears pop. Before long they were so high up that the city below looked like a miniature toy town.

As the plane turned away from the setting sun and pointed its nose toward the east, Katie whispered a soft prayer, "Please, Lord, give us a safe, *wonderful* trip." Then she wrote:

Dear Diary,

We're on our way at last. Katie Thompsen has finally taken off for Switzerland, the United Nations—and adventure!

Chapter 2

The Strange Lady

"Excuse me," said a voice with an unfamiliar accent, "May I see that magazine of yours?"

Startled, Katie looked up into the face of the lady sitting next to her. She had wiry blonde hair, all poofed up, and a bright red mouth and spongy cheeks. Her eyes were hidden behind dark glasses. "Anyone who would wear dark glasses on a plane has *got* to have something to hide," Katie had whispered to Beth when she first saw her.

Katie handed her the magazine. "It's all about the United Nations," she said. "I'm trying to learn about it because that's where we're going."

"Katie's father is a foreign correspondent. That's a kind of news reporter," Beth explained. She leaned forward to take a closer look at her friend's seat companion. "He's writing about an important conference—or something."

"It's a Peace Summit," Katie declared importantly. "I keep telling Beth what it's called and she keeps forgetting," she explained.

Beth shrugged her shoulders. "I'm not interested in Peace Summits. I'm going to visit every pastry shop I can find—just imagine, *real* French pastries! Then I'm going to climb to the top of the Alps and sing, 'The hills are alive, with the sound of music,' at the top of my voice." She threw out her arms as she sang, nearly whacking her friend's nose.

Katie giggled. "You're really crazy, you know that?"

Glancing at the woman next to her, Katie saw she was reading the article on the Peace Summit with interest. Her big, strong hands clutched at the magazine, crumpling the pages. She didn't even look up when the stewardess offered her a snack. *Oh bore, why did I have to get stuck next to her?* Katie thought.

She was relieved when she got to switch places with Beth. By now it was night time, and the cabin lights had been turned off. Most of the passengers were asleep. In front of them her father and Peter were curled up like pretzels under their blankets. Her mother was reading by the little light above her head.

Katie tapped her on the arm. "When will we ever get there? I feel like I've been sitting forever!"

Her mother peeked between the seats and smiled. "This is the most relaxation I've had in months. I'm enjoying myself!"

Closing her eyes, Katie put her head on Beth's shoulder. Next to them the strange lady snored loudly. Beth groaned. "Let me out of here. I'm telling you, I'm going to jump out!"

When they finally drifted off to sleep, it was only to be soon awakened by the stewardess, telling them to fasten their seat belts for landing.

"Wow, look at that!" Peter cried.

Katie rubbed her eyes and tried to focus on the fast approaching earth. Between the billowing clouds she could see towering church steeples and the green of fields and villages. Majestic mountains rose above a beautiful valley, and beyond was the rim of a vast lake, sparkling in the sun.

"The Jura Mountains, and Lake Geneva," her father informed them. Katie wasn't in the mood for a geography lesson. She knew she must look like a mess, but she didn't care. All she wanted was to get off that plane!

A few minutes later the stewardess was saying good-bye at the door. "I hope you had a pleasant flight," she said.

"Good-bye," said Katie and Beth together as they stepped into the sunshine. A few deep breaths and a big stretch and they felt much better.

"Stay close to me," ordered Mr. Thompsen. "We have to collect our suitcases and then we'll be on our way."

Suddenly, Katie nudged Beth. "Look. There she is again."

The blonde woman with the sunglasses was shaking hands with two very important looking men in dark suits and hats.

"Would you believe that?" exclaimed Katie, as they watched the woman being led out of the sliding glass doors and up to a waiting limousine. She squashed herself inside and was driven away.

It wasn't until they had collected their bags, driven to their hotel in a taxi and collapsed exhausted in their room that Katie remembered that the blonde lady had never returned her magazine.

Chapter 3

Bathrooms and Bedbugs

Katie and Beth had a room to themselves
on the third floor of the Beau Rivage Hotel. Katie's
parents and Peter were right next door. The first
thing the two girls did was to fling open their
window and look outside.

It was 6 o'clock on a glorious summer
evening. Beneath them, people hurried home
from work and horns honked impatiently—just
like they did back home in California on a Friday
night. But everything else was different. The
streets were winding and narrow and the cars
all looked tiny compared to the automobiles and
trucks that everyone drove in the United States.

Opposite their hotel, the street was lined
with small shops. The buildings, one attached
to the next like sausage links, must have been
standing for hundreds of years.

"Look over there," said Katie. "The place of your dreams." She pointed to an inviting shop with a yellow and white striped awning and little tables and chairs on the sidewalk. The sign above the door read "Patisserie."

"Chocolate eclairs, cream puffs, petit fours, here I come!" said Beth. Then she yawned and fell back into a waiting chair. "Maybe tomorrow. I'm *so* tired."

There was a sharp knock and the door opened, revealing Peter's grinning face. "Some place, eh?" he said. "Dad wants you to come over to our room. He's got a lot of orders to give."

Next door, Katie and Beth stretched out on the Thompsens' double bed and waited expectantly. Peter seemed happy with his bed in the corner. There was a curtain he could pull across in front, an arrangement which seemed almost better than having his own room. He could pretend it was a secret hide-away.

Mr. Thompsen smiled broadly at everyone. "Well, here we are," he said. "I think we should first of all thank the Lord for bringing us here in safety." He bowed his head and prayed and everyone said an enthusiastic "Amen."

"We came a day early so we would be able to do some sight-seeing," he explained. "Tomorrow we can walk through the city and perhaps see a bit of the countryside as well. Make sure you wear your tennis shoes."

"Be prepared for a lot of walking on this trip," warned Mrs. Thompsen. "We'll also be taking an all-day hike in the Alps later on in the week, so tomorrow will be a good chance for us to get in shape."

"Dinner is at seven tonight," continued Mr. Thompsen. "No jeans. And by the way, muesli's on the menu."

"Muesli? But that's a breakfast cereal," exclaimed Beth.

"Not here it isn't. It was developed by a Swiss doctor as the complete and perfect food for children."

"Well, if it's good for you, it can't taste . . ."

"That's enough, Peter. It's delicious. You'll see."

15

After supper Peter followed Katie and Beth back to their room. "Wait 'til you see the bathroom," he grinned. "especially the toilet."

"Oh, get lost, Pete," said Katie.

Katie and Beth put on their pajamas and bathrobes and set out to investigate the bathroom. Armed with tooth brushes, toothpaste, soap and towels, they headed down the dark hall. At the end were two doors, the one on the right marked "WC," and the one on the left marked "Salle de Bain."

"Let's try the one on the left first," whispered Katie.

As she reached out to turn the handle, the door popped opened. The two girls jumped back, startled.

"It's only me," said Peter, sticking out his tongue. "What did you think I was—a ghost? That's the bathroom, and the other one is the toilet. It has a chain that you have to pull to flush it. Really weird."

As Peter headed off down the hall he added, "Oh! I forgot. You know what Mom found in her bed? A bedbug!" He ran back and stuck his closed fist in front of their faces. "And it looked like this—!" Beth screamed as he opened his fist. There was nothing inside.

"You little creep! You're going to wake everyone up!" Katie gave him a good push and
slammed the door.

"Just be glad you don't have a little brother,"
she said to Beth as they scrubbed their faces.
"They're the worst—and they think they know
everything!"

Soon the girls were scampering back down the hall, giggling and whispering.

Katie jumped into bed, startled when it creaked loudly. *I'm much too excited to close my eyes*, she thought. *Everything's so strange, so different.* But the moment she pulled up the covers and her head touched the soft pillow, she was fast asleep.

Chapter 4

A Worried Scientist

Beth yawned, rolled over and opened one eye. Katie was sitting up in bed, writing in her diary.

"Sorry if I woke you up, but it *is* 7 o'clock," said Katie. "I don't want to forget all the important things that are happening. Some day, when I'm old—maybe not until I'm dead—my diaries will be famous."

Beth yawned again and sat up, her wavy hair sticking out in every direction. "Did you write something about me? Can I read it?"

Quickly, Katie shut the diary. "*Nobody* can read it!"

"Oh, yeah?" said Beth, jumping out of bed and grabbing for the little book.

Katie screamed and rolled over, falling onto

the floor. She just managed to lock the diary before Beth snatched it from her hands.

"Give it back!" she demanded.

A knock on the door and Mrs. Thompsen's voice calling, "Breakfast!" put an end to the squabble.

Beth's eyes lit up. "Breakfast! Yummy!" She tossed the diary back to Katie. "You'd better let me read it, though. I'm your best friend!"

"Maybe," said Katie, "but not until I say so!"

After a breakfast of orange juice, crusty French bread and yogurt, they were ready to explore Geneva.

"How come they speak French here and not Swiss?" asked Peter as they walked down the narrow street in front of their hotel.

Mr. Thompsen laughed. "There's no such language as 'Swiss.' " he explained. "Switzerland is divided into three separate parts, or Cantons as they call them, and in each part they speak a different language: German, French and Italian. We're in the French part."

"Don't they have problems if they can't understand each other?" Katie wondered aloud.

"But they do. Children are required to learn all three languages," her father answered. "And, although each Canton speaks a different language and has its own culture, they're all very proud to be Swiss."

There was a pause while Mrs. Thompsen studied the street map. "Let's see, we'll go up through the old city and visit the Cathedral and Park of the Reformers, then go down to the lake."

All morning they walked through the narrow streets, exclaiming at the beautiful sights. By noon they were hot and hungry and badly in need of a place to rest their tired feet.

Back through the winding, cobblestoned avenues of the old city they wandered, down to the shore of the lake. Greeted by a gentle breeze and a colorful view of sailboats and sun-dappled water, they collapsed with relief on the terrace of an inviting restaurant.

"A turkey sandwich," Katie had just finished ordering when she heard her father say, "Well, my goodness!" in a loud, surprised voice.

Mr. Thompsen pushed back his chair and stood up, waving his arms. "Andrei, Andrei!" he called.

A man walking along the promenade in front of the restaurant stopped suddenly, looked this way and that, then spotted Mr. Thompsen. His face lit up and he came over to join them at their table.

"John Thompsen!" he cried, speaking with a strong foreign accent. The two men shook hands enthusiastically.

"This is an old friend, Dr. Andrei Kopolov. He's a great Russian scientist," Mr. Thompsen explained as he introduced everyone.

Katie winced when he shook her hand. *He might be skinny,* she thought, *but, ow—my poor fingers!*

"Wow!" exclaimed Peter. "A real Russian scientist! Do you have a tail?"

"A tail!" shrieked Beth, then clapped her hand over her mouth.

Dr. Kopolov looked confused.

"A tail is a secret agent who follows you around. You know, like the KGB," Peter said dramatically.

Dr. Kopolov nodded his head in understanding. Putting his finger to his mouth he whispered loudly, "Shh . . . they are *everywhere*. Do you not see those two men over there?" He pointed to a couple of big, burly fellows standing just beyond the row of tables. "Wherever I go, *they* follow me."

Peter stared with round eyes. But Katie and Beth noticed that Dr. Kopolov's eyes twinkled when he spoke and that he winked at Mr. Thompsen.

Katie's father laughed. "Actually, those two men are probably your body guards. Isn't that right?"

Andrei Kopolov nodded his head. "Body guards, yes. They keep me safe, from what, I cannot imagine! They also, unfortunately, keep me prisoner!"

Suddenly, Dr. Kopolov gasped and his face turned pale. He got up quickly, tripping over his chair. "Excuse me, please. I must be going. Yes, well...good-bye!" And he hurried off.

"That was odd," said Mrs. Thompsen.

"Indeed," added Mr. Thompsen, with a puzzled look. "He seemed—frightened."

Beth grabbed Katie's arm and whispered frantically in her ear, "Look!"

Dr. Kopolov had just made his way beyond the row of tables, and with one last worried look over his shoulder, he was swallowed up by a group of Japanese tourists. Behind him came the two big body guards, and following them—

"Oh!" said Katie in surprise as she saw a

familiar figure with dark glasses and poofy blonde hair. Today her mouth wasn't red but bright pink, to match her hot pink dress and handbag. When Dr. Kopolov disappeared into the crowd, the woman stood up on her tip-toes and craned her neck, trying to see over their heads. Then she motioned angrily to the two men beside her— the same ones who had picked her up at the airport—and together they hurried after the scientist.

Chapter 5

A Real Chateau

After lunch, everyone boarded a bus for a
tour of lakeside villages and the famous Chateau
de Chillon.

"A real castle!" exclaimed Peter. "Mom! You've
got to take a picture of me right in front of it,
or Ryan and Jeff will never believe it. Wow! Will
they be jealous!"

Katie looked out of the bus window and tried
to concentrate on the scenery whizzing past.
Instead, she kept seeing the worried face of
Dr. Kopolov.

"Who do you suppose that woman is—and
why did she scare Dr. Kopolov?" Katie
wondered.

Beth shrugged her shoulders. "Beats me.
But I don't like her. She gives me the creeps!"

Katie frowned and tugged on her long
ponytail, thinking hard. "Maybe she's a spy!"
she said. "Maybe she's after him because he's
selling secrets to America. Maybe she's going to
kill him!"

Beth unwrapped a stick of gum and put it
into her mouth. "Could be," she murmured,
sounding unconvinced. "But spies don't wear
hot pink, do they? Maybe she's his wife."

Katie looked at her friend scornfully. "Don't
you have *any* imagination? Honestly!—his *wife*?
Besides, who says spies can't wear pink?"

"Well, *I* don't know!" said Beth. "Ooh, look.
There's the castle!"

Dr. Kopolov and his troubles were forgotten
as the two girls glued their noses to the window.

"Fan*tas*tic!" cried Katie ecstatically as she
jumped off the bus.

The majestic chateau stood atop a rocky reef,
almost entirely surrounded by water. "It was built
in 1150 A.D.," Katie's father told them. "And its
dungeons held many famous prisoners."

"Let's see the dungeons first," Peter said.

Walking through the damp and gloomy
chambers beneath the castle it was easy to imagine
the hopeless despair of its prisoners.

"Look children," said Mr. Thompsen. "See this stone pillar? This is where one of Chillon's most famous prisoners was chained. His name was Bonnivard. His unhappy fate inspired the poet Byron to write a poem about him hundreds of years later. See, here's Byron's name, chiseled into the pillar."

Mrs. Thompsen touched the cold stone softly with her hand. "Do you know, he was so lonely that he made friends with the spiders? And from where he was chained he could just barely catch a glimpse of the lake—and freedom—through that window."

Katie, Beth and Peter looked up. Cut out of the thick wall was a small rectangular opening which framed a lovely view of the lake and the Alps beyond.

On the ride back to Geneva, Katie sat next to her father. She wanted to talk to him about Dr. Kopolov. Trying to remember all the details, she told him how she had first seen the strange lady on the plane and how, later, the woman had seemed to be following the scientist.

"Well, perhaps she did scare him in some way," said Mr. Thompsen thoughtfully. "But I can't imagine why. I hope he isn't in some kind of trouble. He'll be joining us next week when we hike in the Alps. We can find out then."

"There's something fishy going on, that's for sure," Katie said with conviction.

Her father smiled. "You'll make a fine journalist one day, Katie. You can smell a story a mile away!"

After they had returned to the hotel and had a short rest, Mr. Thompsen informed the family that they were going to a small country restaurant for dinner.

While they waited for their taxi to arrive, Mrs. Thompsen took the girls into a shop to buy postcards. Katie and Beth picked out a few nice ones and went to the counter to pay with their Swiss francs.

"What's this?" Katie asked her mother, pointing to a little money box on the counter.

"Oh, that's for contributions to help the poor children," she explained. "Only the money isn't used to buy food or clothing. It's to buy skis! The Swiss have the firm belief that every child, no matter how poor, should own a pair of skis!"

They raced back across the street to the waiting taxi. Soon they were out of the city and winding through the lush, green countryside.

"So where's the restaurant?" Peter asked when the taxi stopped in front of what looked like a barn. Chickens clucked in the yard and they could hear cow bells in the distance.

"This *is* the restaurant," said Mr. Thompsen. "Follow me and you'll see."

Entering through a plain wooden door, they found themselves inside a charming room scattered with tables covered by red and white checked tablecloths. Seated in one area was a large group of noisy mountain climbers who had probably been hiking all day. They wore traditional lederhosen (leather shorts with suspenders) and hiking boots. Big and strong,

with rosy cheeks and laugh-crinkled eyes, they filled the room with good cheer.

"Fondue for five," Mr. Thompsen ordered after they had been seated.

When the waiter set a pot of bubbling cheese over a candle warmer, and placed a basket of bread chunks at each end of the table, Peter objected indignantly, "Is that *all*? I'm starving!"

"Grab a fork and dig in," his mother laughed. "You'll soon fill up."

In an instant five forks jabbed five cubes of bread. Then they all collided as they tried to dunk their forkfuls into the pot one at a time.

"Hey, you knocked mine off," Peter wailed to no one in particular.

"Ooh, gross," Beth cried as she tried to get her tongue around a gooey thread of cheese trailing from the pot to her fork.

Suddenly they were aware of the silence from the next table, then a jolly laugh. One of the climbers jumped up and came over to their table.

"Here, let me show you," he offered. Grabbing Katie's fork he speared a chunk of bread, swirled it expertly around in the bubbling cheese and lifted it to Katie's mouth with a flourish.

"Bon appetit, ma cherie," he laughed.

Soon they were all jabbing, dipping and twirling like experts. When the apple strudel arrived, even Peter declared it the best meal ever.

By this time the mountain climbers had begun singing traditional mountain songs. Many of the other guests joined in. Mr. Thompsen knew some of the tunes and was applauded loudly when he sang along. Soon serenading hikers surrounded their table and Katie and Beth were laughing so hard they almost choked on their strudel. When

Peter offered to sing Yankee Doodle Dandy, Katie forgot to be embarrassed and Beth offered to join in.

"That was the *most* fun I've ever had," Beth declared as she tumbled into bed that night.

"Hmmm . . ." Katie mumbled as she turned off the light. Her eyes closed, and she was soon fast asleep.

But what was this? *Andrei Kopolov was desperately pushing his way through a sea of tourists. Everyone was taking pictures at once, and each time the bulbs flashed Katie saw his frightened face lit up like a scary mask. Marching behind him was a huge poof of wiry blonde hair.*

"Wait. . . . Stop!" cried Katie, tossing and turning in her sleep. *Dr. Kopolov had backed up against the edge of a cliff. He took one step too many and fell over—right into a giant swirling pot of fondue.*

Chapter 6

Watch Out!

The next morning Beth woke up first. When Katie opened her eyes she saw her friend peering out the window.

"It's raining," Beth said gloomily. "How can it rain in the middle of July?"

Katie rolled out of bed and began rummaging through the closet. "I had the strangest dream. All about Dr. Kopolov and that spy lady and a huge pot of bubbling fondue."

"You must have eaten too much last night. I ate piles, but I'm still hungry today! I know— let's ask your parents if we can go to the Patisserie for breakfast," Beth said excitedly. "We still haven't had any pastries and I'm dying to try them all!"

Grabbing umbrellas, the two girls raced down the hall and told Katie's mother their plan.

"Well, I don't see why not," she said. "Your father had to attend a conference early this morning and we'll be meeting him at the United Nations later on."

Le Petit Chat, the little cafe across the street, was the perfect antidote for a rainy morning. Inside they found round marble-topped tables and brass chairs with gold velvet cushions. A huge mirror hung on the wall in a gilded frame. Customers sat quietly, drinking special coffees and reading the morning paper. Others talked among themselves, discussing the affairs of the day.

Beth made a beeline for the counter where the pastries were displayed. She chose an enormous chocolate eclair *and* a chocolate-filled croissant.

"Boy, are you a pig," Peter mumbled back at the table, his mouth full of Black Forest pastry. "Even I couldn't eat all that!"

"Is that so?" asked Mrs. Thompsen, looking amused. "When you learn to take smaller bites, we might believe you."

Beth daintily placed a piece of eclair in her

mouth and rolled her eyes in ecstasy. "This is heaven, absolute heaven!"

Katie sampled her apricot tart and nodded her head approvingly. "I think we'll definitely have to make a trip back here this evening."

"And tomorrow morning, and tomorrow night, and—" Beth continued.

"Wait a minute," said Mrs. Thompsen. "we *do* have other things to do besides eat, you know. Thank goodness the rain has stopped. Now we can walk to the United Nations without getting soaked."

It was almost a mile, but everyone felt they needed the exercise after their rather unusual breakfast. Everyone, that is, except Beth. "Ow, my stomach," she groaned after they had been walking about 10 minutes. "Why, oh why did I eat all that horrible stuff?"

"We'll go back tonight and have some more," Katie teased. "And tomorrow, and the next day—"

"Oh, be quiet," snapped Beth. "I never want to see another pastry as long as I live!"

Twenty minutes later Mr. Thompsen could be seen waving to them from in front of the long white United Nations building. "What kept you?" he asked. "I've been waiting almost half an hour."

Three pairs of eyes looked at Beth, who had collapsed gratefully onto a bench. "Beth isn't feeling well, so we had to walk slowly. We tried to find a taxi but they were all taken," Katie's mother explained.

"But you're almost better now, right?" Katie asked, putting her arm around her friend.

Beth nodded. "I think so," she said hopefully.

"Let's all sit down for a minute while I explain a few things," suggested Mr. Thompsen.

"This building," he began, gesturing behind him, "called the Palais des Nations, stands for peace and unity among the nations. The United Nations was created after World War II and has representatives from almost all the countries of the world. At the moment, leaders from the United States and the Soviet Union are meeting here to discuss future plans for maintaining peace and understanding between our countries."

"Is that why Dr. Kopolov is here?" Katie asked.

Her father nodded. "Yes. He's giving an important speech this morning." Mr. Thompsen looked at his watch. "In fact, I'm due there now. Unfortunately, you aren't allowed in the meetings, but you can walk around the building if you wish."

Mr. Thompsen hurried away. "Well," said Katie's mother, looking after him. "That was a short visit. I don't think we'll be seeing much of him until dinner time."

"Katie, why don't you sit here with Beth until she's feeling better, and I'll take Peter inside, that is, if I can, with all these important meetings going on."

Katie and Beth sat quietly on the bench, hoping it wouldn't start raining again. The sky had turned ominously dark and they could hear thunder in the distance.

"This has *not* been my favorite day," complained Beth. "I wouldn't mind lying in my own bed right now—with my cat! She must miss me a lot."

The two girls contented themselves with counting the limousines and other fancy cars that pulled up in front of the Palais des Nations and watching who got out of them. The front of the building was lined with security guards and reporters. Katie stood up on the bench so she could see better.

"Oh, there's Dr. Kopolov," she cried excitedly.

Beth pulled on Katie's pant-leg. "Look over there," she hissed. "There's someone hiding in the bushes."

From her vantage point on the bench, Katie could clearly see the form of a woman concealed behind some foliage less than a hundred yards away. It was impossible to mistake the woman for any other than—"The spy lady!" cried Katie in disbelief. "I don't believe it—not again!"

Sure enough, there she was. Today she wore a yellow rain coat and hat and shiny black galoshes over her shoes. She peered intently from behind the bushes as Dr. Kopolov got out of the car and paused to speak with the journalists. Then she looked carefully this way and that—and spotted the two girls. Her eyes narrowed as she stared at them, and Katie held her breath, hoping that the woman wouldn't pull out a gun. Perhaps her umbrella was really some kind of weapon! Katie sighed with relief when the woman turned away.

"Did you see her mean face? And this time she wasn't wearing sunglasses!" said Katie.

"She's probably just nearsighted," Beth returned. "Nearsighted people always look mean when they're trying to see who you are."

"Oh, Beth! What's she doing now?"

Quietly, the woman stepped out from behind the bushes and started walking toward Andrei Kopolov and the crowd of journalists.

Katie grabbed her friend's arm. "Let's follow her."

The two girls crept after the bright yellow figure until they were close enough to hear what the scientist was saying. "And so," he concluded, smiling to the crowd, "I am hoping to inspire scientists everywhere to use their knowledge for peaceful purposes. . . ."

Her eyes narrow and her mouth set in a determined, thin red line, the blonde lady reached into her handbag.

Katie had to think fast. She grabbed the woman's arm and started yelling, "Kopolov—watch out!"

Instantly they were surrounded by an army of security guards. Strong arms held the struggling blur of yellow in a steely grip. The woman's purse smashed to the ground, throwing its contents onto the wet pavement. Katie looked frantically for something that resembled a weapon . . . but there was nothing.

"Please! Let me go!" cried the blonde lady, flushed and frightened.

Katie was suddenly aware that everyone was
staring at her. Feeling the color rise from her neck
to her cheeks, she wished she could sink into
the ground and die.

"Well, I . . . , well, she . . ." was all Katie could
manage to say.

Chapter 7

Saying Good-bye

Later that evening, Katie still hadn't recovered from her disastrous experience. She sat on her bed in the hotel and stared at her feet.

"This is the most terrible thing that has ever, in my whole entire life, happened to me," she wailed. "Oooh—when I think of what I *did!*" She pounded the bed furiously.

Beth shook her head sympathetically. "It's not your fault. You had no idea. You simply looked at all the evidence and came up with what *you* thought was the proper conclusion. So what if you were wrong? Everyone's wrong sometimes."

There was a knock on the door and Beth went to open it.

"Not in bed yet?" asked Mrs. Thompsen, coming to sit next to Katie and putting her arm around her shoulder.

"Oh, Mom, how could I have been so stupid?" cried Katie. "My life is ruined!"

"As bad as all that, is it? I know it must seem that way right now. But you were only trying to do what you thought was right. It took some courage to stand up like that. You thought you were protecting Dr. Kopolov."

"Yeah, and all I did was make a fool of myself. I'll never stand up for anyone ever again!"

"Now, you know you don't mean that," her mother said soothingly. "You're just suffering from wounded pride. Doing the right thing sometimes involves risks, you know."

"Oh, I know," Katie answered, sniffling a little, a tiny smile appearing on her lips. "It *was* kind of funny. Imagine, thinking she was reaching for a gun, when all she was doing was reaching for a handkerchief to blow her nose and wipe her eyes."

Beth started to laugh, then Mrs. Thompsen, and finally Katie joined in. "This is one episode I'll definitely have to include in my diary. Some day I'll have to prove to my grandchildren that it really did happen!"

Mrs. Thompsen tucked her daughter into bed and turned off the light. "When we go on our hike tomorrow you'll have the chance to get to know your mystery woman better. We're all looking forward to that chance. But for now, good-night."

The stars were still shining when the two girls jumped out of bed the next morning. The chilly air made them shiver as they quickly got dressed, throwing warm sweaters over their short sleeved tops.

"Now we get to see the *real* Switzerland," said Beth as they raced downstairs. "Hurray for the Alps!"

The family tumbled into the waiting bus and sped off into the rising sun and their last adventure before returning home. As they rode toward the mountains the lovely countryside slowly took shape before them, illuminated by the brightening sunshine. Closer and closer they came to the glittering white peak of Monte Blanc.

"Bonjour, bonjour!" they were greeted enthusiastically by Dr. Kopolov when they got off the bus.

Katie cringed at the sight of the black limousine and the blonde lady approaching them. This was the moment she had been dreading.

"My dear friends!" said Dr. Kopolov, giving each one a hug. "You remember my sister, Alenka

Hanover, from yesterday. I'm sorry you didn't meet under more pleasant circumstances." He gave Katie a warm smile.

How different Mrs. Hanover seemed, now that Katie knew she wasn't a spy! Her hair was still poofy, her cheeks were still spongy, and in her bright purple pants and green alpiner hat she looked stranger than ever. But her manner no longer seemed menacing.

Smiling broadly at everyone, Mrs. Hanover cried, "Thank you so much for asking me to join you. It is one of my favorite things, you know, to hike in the Alps. Ahh!" Dramatically, she flung her arms wide, then threw them around Katie and kissed her on the cheek. "We will have a nice long chat. Now—up the mountain we go!"

"Keep your eyes open for wild strawberries and blueberries," called Mr. Thompsen.

"You see, my dear," began Mrs. Hanover, puffing along beside Katie, "I left the Soviet Union long ago and came to America. Ever since then, I have tried to convince Andrei to leave as well." She snorted and stomped her feet. "That brother of mine is stubborn! I say to him, 'But Andrei, in America you will be free. You can say and do what you want without fear. You can become rich—as I have done!' Does he listen to me? Not a bit! So, I come to Switzerland. I try to convince him. I make his life miserable, arguing with him, following him everywhere with my chauffeur and secretary. It is no wonder you thought I was a spy!"

She paused for a moment to wipe her forehead and catch her breath. She looked sadly after her brother. He and the Thompsens were way ahead of them. His arms were waving as he talked and sometimes he stopped for emphasis.

"I realize now that I will never change his mind," Mrs. Hanover said. She pointed behind them and Katie saw the two bodyguards following at a discreet distance. "That is the kind of thing Andrei has to live with. I worry about him so much, although he assures me life has improved in the Soviet Union."

"But why doesn't he want to leave?" asked Katie.

"Yeah," added Beth. "The United States is the best place in the whole world! He must be crazy not to want to live there!"

Alenka Hanover laughed her loud and booming laugh. "It might surprise you to know that most people think their country is the best in the world. But why don't you ask *him* that question? I think he could answer better than I."

"Hey, look!" shouted Peter "There's a mountain goat!"

"Yes! And there's another one!" cried Beth.

Peter ran off the trail and into the bushes, chasing after the animals.

"Where's Peter disappeared to?" Mrs. Thompsen called sharply a moment later.

"I'm over here!" came a distant voice. "Wait 'til you see all the strawberries I've found!" Peter reappeared suddenly from behind the trees, his hands filled with tiny bright red berries.

"Yummy!" said Katie and Beth. "They're so sweet!"

Walking on a bit farther, they found that the forest ended and they stood on the edge of an alpine meadow. Ringed by trees and shaped like a giant bowl, it sloped gently down on all sides. In the middle was a tiny lake.

"Oh, it's lovely," breathed Mrs. Thompsen. "We can have our picnic over there." She pointed down toward the lake.

Katie, Beth and Peter left the others far behind as they raced down the hillside to the edge of the water. They picked out a spot to lay the blankets and waited eagerly for Mr. Thompsen and the picnic basket to arrive.

Never before had a picnic lunch tasted so delicious! The chicken, French bread, pickles,

cheese, apricots and tomatoes were finished off
in no time.

"Did you know that the pine trees surround-
ing this meadow are very special?" asked Mr.
Kopolov. "In the spring they bloom with
thousands of flaming red flowers and look as
if they are on fire."

Katie stared at the trees, trying to imagine
herself ringed by flaming flowers. Sighing
contentedly, she lay back on the blanket and gazed
up at the bright blue sky. *I want to remember this
moment forever*, she thought. *Tomorrow we'll be going
home and it will all seem like a dream.*

"Andrei," Mrs. Hanover was saying, "Katie
and Beth have something they would like to ask you."

Katie sat up and looked at Beth. Shaking
her head, Beth motioned for Katie to explain.

"Well," said Katie, a trifle embarrassed. "We
don't really understand why you want to stay
in the Soviet Union when you could live in the
United States."

Andrei Kopolov became thoughtful. "I will
tell you a story which I hope will make you
understand. There was once a boy who lived in
a small, poor village. His life was hard but he
was happy, surrounded by his family and people

who loved him. On the other side of a raging river was a beautiful city where people lived in great luxury.

One day the boy was playing by the river and he found a magic stone. When he picked it up, a shining bridge appeared that could take him across to the other side. At the same moment, a voice spoke to him saying that the stone had another purpose. He could use it to help bring peace to the people of his village. But if he chose to do this, he could never cross the bridge and live in the beautiful city. Tell me, how would *you* decide if you were that boy?"

"I guess I would have to stay and help my village. Though it *would* be tempting to cross the river," said Katie.

"Exactly so," replied Andrei Kopolov. "I am just like that boy. God gave me a special gift, my scientific knowledge, and this I try to use to help my people. In the past I was put in prison because I refused to use my knowledge to build evil weapons. But now the government is at last listening to my voice and to others who believe the same. I am so thankful God gave me the strength all these years to stand firm in what I believe and not to give in to pressure or temptation."

Alenka Hanover wagged her finger at the thin, determined man beside her. "What can one do with such a brother? I cannot argue when he speaks like this. I can only feel ashamed that my faith is not as strong."

The lovely afternoon came to an end all too soon. As they hiked back toward the waiting bus, Katie knew the time had come to say good-bye to her new friends.

"I will never forget you," she said earnestly to Dr. Kopolov, giving him a big hug. "I hope

we can see you again one day."

"I hope so, too, my young friend," the scientist said with a smile.

Sniffling noisily, Alenka Hanover eased herself into the waiting limousine. "Oh, where are my sunglasses!" she said, rummaging through her purse. "When I start to cry, I always put them on," she explained. "I wore them almost all the way here on the plane—and I shall probably wear them almost all the way back!"

As the long, black vehicle began to pull away, Mrs. Hanover's arm shot out of the window and she thrust a crumpled roll of papers into Katie's hand. "The magazine—on the plane—I for-got...." Her voice faded away as the car picked up speed.

Katie waved until the last bit of wind-blown blonde hair could no longer be seen. Then she climbed onto the bus and sat down beside her brother.

"Ow!" he said angrily. "You're squashing me. And your giant foot is on my toe!"

"Sorry," she answered absently, huddling into the corner.

The setting sun cast a crimson glow as they wound their way down the mountain. Tomorrow they would be home again, and Switzerland—with its adventure, castles, Alps, lakes and meadows—would be only a memory.

Yet Katie hoped it would be much more than just a memory. She wanted her experiences to live on in her life forever. Somehow, she felt sure they would.

Dear Diary,

I cannot believe how this trip has turned out! Here I am on the plane going back home. I haven't been away for very long, but I feel like a different person! How will I ever explain all my experiences to my friends? Will they ever understand? Well, at least Beth was there with me. She'll understand even if the rest of the world doesn't.

Mr. Somonov... Mrs. Hanover... Two such different people, but part of the same family. Sort of like me and Peter, I guess! It just goes to show that you can't tell everything from a person's looks.

I thought Alenka Hanover was a spy. Boy, did I mess up!! She was really a nice person, even though she was a bit too worried about all the wrong things-- like money and big cars, and having her own way.

Then there's Andrei Somonov--he really has a different idea about what is important! I wish I could be just like him someday- smart and with a strong faith. Even though it's been hard, he's followed God's will in his life. He's a great Christian example, not only to his sister and his friends, but to his country! Why, he's a great example to the entire world!

When I get home, you know the first thing I'm going to do? I'm going to ride my bike up the hill behind our house, to where I can see the whole valley, and I'm going to think really hard about everything that's happened. That way I won't forget what I've learned. Maybe I'll never be a Christian example to my whole country, or the world, but I can at least start, with Jesus' help, with my family and friends.

Then, after I'm finished thinking, I'm going to eat a HUGE piece of apple pie, because Mom promised she'd bake one when we got home!

And here's something else that's really wonderful. Dad said maybe, just maybe, he might take us on another trip someday. I can hardly wait! Just think of all the amazing places there are to visit. And all the fantastic things there are to learn!!

P.S. I think I use the word think too much!